by Sazaklis

THE HOPPING HERO

illustrated by
Art Baltazar

Starring...

HOPPY
THE MARVEL BUNNY

SOBEK

MR MIND

TAWKY TAWNY

CONTENTS

SUPER-PET HERO FILE 007:
HOPPY

ultra-hearing

wisdom

flight

super-strength

courage

super-speed

Super hero owner:
CAPTAIN MARVEL

Species: Bunny
Place of Birth: Animalville
Age: Unknown
Favourite food: Carrots

Bio: One day, Hoppy spoke the magic word "Shazam!" and gained the same superpowers as his hero, Captain Marvel.

SUPER-PET ENEMY FILE 007:
SOBEK

razor-sharp teeth

super-strength

razor-sharp claws

Super-villain owner:
BLACK ADAM

SUPER-PET ENEMY FILE 007B:
MR MIND

super intelligence

mind control

voice transmitter

Super-villain partner:
DR SIVANA

SHAZAM!

On a sunny day, **Hoppy** the bunny met two of his friends at the Fawcett City Animal Festival.

Millie the rabbit wanted to enjoy the rides, attractions, and games. **Tawky Tawny** the tiger looked forward to all the food.

"Thanks for spending the day with me," Hoppy said to his friends. "It's nice to relax and have a little fun."

"Ooh, look!" Millie pointed to a nearby game. "Let's see if Hoppy is as strong as Marvel Bunny!"

Unlike Tawky Tawny, Millie did not know that Hoppy *was* **Marvel Bunny.** Each time Hoppy said the word **"SHAZAM!"**, a bolt of lightning gave him the power of six species. These powers had to be kept secret.

THE WISDOM OF SALAMANDER!

THE POWER OF ZEBREUS!

THE STRENGTH OF HOGULES!

THE COURAGE OF ABALONE!

THE STAMINA OF ANTLERS!

THE SPEED OF MONKURY!

Millie pulled Hoppy over to the game. It was called Test Your Might.

Players used a rubber hammer to whack a metal target. A scale measured each person's strength.

Hoppy blushed. "I don't think that's such a good idea –" he began.

Suddenly, the friends heard screams on the other side of the festival.

The merry-go-round was spinning out of control and falling apart! The horses were flying in all directions.

Little animals clung to the ride. They cried out in fear. Their parents stood frozen in shock. No one could get near the machine without getting hurt.

"Mmm!" said Tawky Tawny, rubbing his tummy. "I sure am hungry!"

"How can you think of food at a time like this?" Millie shouted.

"I'll get some hot dogs!" Hoppy said, running into the empty snack tent.

"Hot dogs? But lives are in danger!" cried Millie. **"Who will help us?"**

In the distance, Tawky Tawny heard the rumble of thunder and the crash of lightning. "Oh, I have a good feeling help is on the way," the tiger replied with a smile.

"SHAZAM!"

In a flash, **Hoppy changed into Marvel Bunny.** He rushed to the rescue.

At the same time, the merry-go-round spun even faster. Tawky Tawny darted on all fours into the path of danger. He tried to control the crowd.

"Everybody back!" the tiger yelled, pushing onlookers with his paws.

Suddenly, one of the horses flew at the crowd. A blur of yellow and pink zoomed by overhead.

WOOOOSH!

Marvel Bunny reined in the plastic stallion. He placed it safely on the ground. Then he saved two baby otters and returned them to their parents.

Suddenly, more parts of the ride broke off. More screams were heard.

A piece of wood had trapped Mr and Mrs Sloth. Tawky Tawny heard their cries and went to help. The tiger lifted the debris off the animals, placed them on his back, and ran to safety.

Tawky Tawny ran faster and faster as the rubble got closer and closer.

Meanwhile, Marvel Bunny sped over to the merry-go-round's controls. The power switch had been broken off. He could not shut off the machine!

Using his gift of wisdom, Marvel Bunny reached under the controls. He started taking apart the engine. His paws moved at super-speed. Soon, a flurry of gears and bolts littered the ground around him.

SKREEEECH!

The crumbling machine finally slowed to a stop. Marvel Bunny zipped around. He brought each crying child back to his or her parents.

Then Marvel Bunny landed next to Tawky Tawny. **"Phew!"** the hero sighed. **"I'm glad that's over."**

Tawky Tawny leaned against a plastic horse that had escaped the merry-go-round. "Indeed," he replied. "Too much horseplay for my taste!"

"Someone must have messed with the controls," Marvel Bunny said.

Millie hopped over. "Oh, gosh!" she said, blushing. "Marvel Bunny! Here! I must thank you!"

Millie closed her eyes and puckered her lips. She leaned in for a kiss.

"Um, if you'll excuse me," the hero said, turning redder than his uniform. "I have a job to finish."

He flew into the sky as Millie fell forward and smooched the horse!

Moments later, Hoppy returned with the hot dogs. As he walked over to his friends, something caught his eye.

A crocodile tail disappeared behind a tent. When Hoppy turned the corner, the tail and its owner were gone!

"**This can't be!**" the bunny said.

Just then, Hoppy's friends spotted him. Millie was very excited. She could not stop talking about Marvel Bunny. Tawky Tawny took his hot dog from Hoppy. He swallowed it in one gulp and passed Millie hers.

"Thanks, but no thanks," she said. "I'm too excited to eat. Did you see Marvel Bunny? **He's so dreamy!**"

Tawky Tawny helped himself to Millie's hot dog as well.

Then Tawky Tawny put his paw on Hoppy's shoulder. "What's the matter, dear friend?" he asked.

"I can't eat either," Hoppy said. "I think I saw Sobek."

Tawky Tawny swallowed hard. "That can't be," the tiger said with surprise. "Isn't Sobek the Croc just a myth? No one's actually seen him before!"

Hoppy shook his head. **"He's real,"** he replied. **"And he's up to no good."**

Chapter 2

REPTILE RAIDER

Everyone in Fawcett City had heard stories of **Sobek**. The croc's big sharp teeth often gave children nightmares.

In real life, however, Sobek was simply an oversized scaredy-croc. He was embarrassed by his crooked teeth and ran from his own shadow.

On most days, Sobek hid in the deep, dark sewers. In fact, he did not know why he had come to the Animal Festival or broken the merry-go-round.

When he realized what he had done, Sobek ran away in tears.

Then, suddenly, a tiny voice echoed in his head. "Stop snivelling, you weakling!" the voice commanded. **"Your mind is under my control."**

Sobek stared blankly into the distance. **"Yes, master,"** he replied.

"Go back to that festival and cause more trouble. It's the only way to lure Marvel Bunny into my trap," the voice continued. "Once you are both in my control, **I will create the Monster Society of Evil!**"

Back at the festival everything had returned to normal, but Hoppy was still on edge. He had a feeling that more trouble was on the way.

"Let's get some ice cream to calm our nerves," Tawky Tawny said.

Millie agreed. Together, they walked over to Mr Seal, the ice cream seller.

Without warning, more screams and gasps came from the crowd. Tawky Tawny's hair stood on end. He looked at the fairgrounds and saw ... **Sobek!**

"Can it be?" someone cried.

"He's real, and I knew it,"

Hoppy said, gritting his teeth.

Sobek climbed on to the Ferris wheel.

He waited for the next seat to come his

way. Then he ripped it off its hinges!

The reptile raider snarled and lifted the chair high above his head. With a roar, he hurled it at the innocent animals below.

"Oh no, not again!" Millie cried. She looked over at Hoppy. The bunny was nowhere to be seen.

Hoppy quickly hopped behind the festival's dunk tank and looked around. The coast was clear.

A bolt of lighting changed Hoppy into Marvel Bunny. The hero zoomed over to the Ferris wheel. He caught the falling seat.

WOOOOSH!

In the meantime, Tawky Tawny shook off his coat and glasses. He raced over to the attraction. Marvel Bunny needed his help!

The tiger climbed the Ferris wheel and sneaked up behind Sobek. The croc was busy destroying the ride.

"Relax," Tawky Tawny yelled at Sobek. "And have a seat!"

THWAAACK!

The tiger tackled the crocodile. They tumbled into another seat on the Ferris wheel.

Using his front paws, Tawky Tawny pinned Sobek down on his back. During the struggle, the tiger discovered a small worm sitting on top of Sobek's head.

Tawky Tawny blinked with surprise.

It was **Mr Mind**, Marvel Bunny's enemy! The wicked worm had mind control powers, and despite his size, he had grand plans.

Suddenly, the day's events all made sense. Mr Mind had been controlling Sobek. The crocodile was not able to stop himself.

"It ends here, Mr Mind!" yelled Tawky Tawny, reaching for the worm.

Mr Mind shot a super-strong web, trapping the tiger in a silky bond.

"Throw this troublesome tiger overboard!" Mr Mind yelled to Sobek.

The croc obeyed. He lifted Tawky Tawny over his head.

Ugh! I shouldn't have eaten all those hot dogs, thought Talky Tawny.

Suddenly, the tiger was falling through the air. The ground was rushing up at him.

Tawky Tawny shut his eyes. Certain doom was down below, and those hot dogs were coming back up.

Chapter 3

WICKED WORM

"Need a lift?"

Tawky Tawny heard a voice and opened his eyes. He hovered in the air.

His best friend in the world flew up to save him! Marvel Bunny carried the tiger to an empty Ferris wheel seat.

"Sit tight," said Marvel Bunny. "I must stop Sobek before it's too late."

Sobek growled and grabbed Marvel Bunny in a bear hug.

Down below, Millie was watching with worry. She ran to a kind bird named Doctor Falcon. "You have to get me up there," she pleaded. "They need our help!"

Doctor Falcon agreed. He picked Millie up. Together, they flew up to Tawky Tawny. WHOOSH!

Using teeth and talons, they ripped through his silky bonds.

"Thank you, sir," said the tiger, turning to join the fight.

Meanwhile, Marvel Bunny finally
broke free from Sobek's grasp. The
enemies fell off the Ferris wheel.

They both landed in the dunk tank. The shock broke Sobek out of Mr Mind's spell.

Marvel Bunny caught the wicked worm before he could creep away. "I'm not surprised that you're behind this," said the hero.

"You'll change your tune once you see things my way," Mr Mind replied. **The villain quickly put Marvel Bunny into a trance.**

"Yes, master," the hero replied.

"Together, we will rule the animals

of Fawcett City," added Marvel Bunny.

"All hail the Monster Society of Evil!"

"Great minds think alike!" said

Mr Mind, twitching with evil glee.

"What have you done to my hero!" Millie shouted at Mr Mind.

Her cries broke the villain's focus and his evil spell. Summoning all his powers, Marvel Bunny flew Mr Mind away from the festival.

When they were alone, Marvel Bunny opened his fist and looked at his enemy. "It's time to put an end to your mind games," the hero yelled.

A bolt of lightning ripped through the sky. It blasted them both.

Marvel Bunny was now good old Hoppy. Mr Mind had passed out. A plume of smoke lifted off the worm's antennae. Mr Mind would not remember a thing when he woke up.

In the meantime, Tawky Tawny called the police. When Hoppy returned to the festival, he turned over the worm to the officers.

"Marvel Bunny had to run," said Hoppy, "but he gave me this instruction: 'Lock up Mr Mind where he will have no visitors.' **It's the only way to make his powers useless."**

The police were very careful. They placed the worm inside a lead box with breathing holes. Then they drove off to Fawcett City Jail.

Millie ran over to Hoppy. "Wow!"

she said. "You're so brave! Come on,

I'll buy you some ice cream."

"What about my new friend?" asked

Hoppy, pointing at Sobek.

"The more, the merrier!" said Millie.

Everyone at the festival cheered.

Some of the rides had been damaged, but the day was saved. Seeing Marvel Bunny in action was more exciting than all the amusement parks in Fawcett City combined!

KNOW YOUR HERO PETS

1. Krypto
2. Streaky
3. Beppo
4. Comet
5. Ace
6. Robin Robin
7. Jumpa
8. Whatzit
9. Storm
10. Topo
11. Ark
12. Hoppy
13. Batcow
14. Big Ted
15. Proty
16. Gleek
17. Paw Pooch
18. Bull Dog
19. Chameleon Collie
20. Hot Dog
21. Tail Terrier
22. Tusky Husky
23. Mammoth Mutt
24. Dawg
25. B'dg
26. Stripezoid
27. Zallion
28. Ribitz
29. Bzzd
30. Gratch
31. Buzzoo
32. Fossfur
33. Zhoomp
34. Eeny

1

2

3

4

5

6

7

8

9

10

11

12

13

14

15

16

17

18

19

20

21

22

23

24

25

26

27

28

29

30

31

32

33

34

KNOW YOUR VILLAIN PETS

1. Bizarro Krypto
2. Ignatius
3. Rozz
4. Mechanikat
5. Crackers
6. Giggles
7. Joker Fish
8. Chauncey
9. Artie Puffin
10. Griff
11. Waddles
12. Dogwood
13. Mr. Mind
14. Sobek
15. Misty
16. Sneezers
17. General Manx
18. Nizz
19. Fer-El
20. Titano
21. Bit-Bit
22. X-43
23. Dex-Starr
24. Glomulus
25. Whoosh
26. Pronto
27. Snorrt
28. Rolf
29. Tootz
30. Eezix
31. Donald
32. Waxxee
33. Fimble
34. Webbik

1

2

3

4

5

6

7

8

9

10

11

12

13

14

15

16

17

18

19

20

21

22

23

24

25

26

27

28

29

30

31

32

33

34

JOKES

What kind of books do bunnies read?

No idea.

The ones with hoppy endings!

Why did the bunnies go on strike?

Why?

They wanted a raise in celery!

Why did the bunny go to the barber?

No clue.

He needed a hare cut.

GLOSSARY

debris scattered pieces of something that has been broken

society group of people who share the same interests

species one of the groups into which animals are divided based on common traits

stallion adult male horse

trance feeling of being sleepy and under the control of another

wisdom knowledge, experience, and good judgement

MEET THE AUTHOR

John Sazaklis

John Sazaklis spent part of his life working in a family shop called the House of Doughnuts. The other part, he spent drawing and writing stories. He has illustrated Spider-Man books and written Batman books for HarperCollins.

MEET THE ILLUSTRATOR

Eisner Award-winner Art Baltazar

Art Baltazar defines cartoons and comics not only as a style of art, but as a way of life. Art is the creative force behind *The New York Times* best-selling, Eisner Award-winning, DC Comics series Tiny Titans, and the co-writer for *Billy Batson and the Magic of SHAZAM!* Art draws comics and never has to leave the house. He lives with his lovely wife, Rose, big boy Sonny, little boy Gordon, and little girl Audrey.

ART BALTAZAR says:

Read all the DC SUPER-PETS stories today!

www.raintreepublishers.co.uk
Visit our website to find out
more information about
Raintree books.

To order:
☎ Phone 0845 6044371
🖹 Fax +44 (0) 1865 312263
🖳 Email myorders@raintreepublishers.co.uk

Customers from outside the UK please telephone +44 1865 312262

Raintree is an imprint of Capstone Global Library Limited,
a company incorporated in England and Wales having its registered office at
7 Pilgrim Street, London, EC4V 6LB – Registered company number: 6695582

First published by Picture Window Books in 2012
First published in the United Kingdom in 2012
The moral rights of the proprietor have been asserted.

Art Director and Designer: Bob Lentz
Editors: Donald Lemke and Vaarunika Dharmapala
Creative Director: Heather Kindseth
Editorial Director: Michael Dahl

ISBN 978 1 406 23662 0 (paperback)
16 15 14 13 12
10 9 8 7 6 5 4 3 2 1

British Library Cataloguing in Publication Data
A full catalogue record for this book is available from the British Library.